DATE DUE

APR 2 1975	JE 05 '86 06	
APR 2 1 1975	JY 2 8 '87	
JUN 5	OC 26 '87	
SEP 9 1975	AG 4 '88	
SEP 1 8 1975	SE 9 '88	
	AG 1 '89	
AUG 26 1981	JY 29 '91	
AUG 26 1981	AP 2 9 '93	
OCT. 3 0 1981		
NOV. 5 1981	JUN 0 5	
SEP. 1 8 1982	JA 09 '03	

W9-AKE-208

11,507

Prather, Ray
  No trespassing.   N.Y., Macmillan, [1974]
  unp.   col.illus.

  I.Title.

EAU CLAIRE DISTRICT LIBRARY

No Trespassing

BY RAY PRATHER

MACMILLAN PUBLISHING CO., INC.
New York
COLLIER MACMILLAN PUBLISHERS
London

77693
EAU CLAIRE DISTRICT LIBRARY

Baker and Taylor — 3/5/75 — $4.95

11,501

Copyright © 1974 Ray Prather. All rights reserved. No part of this book
may be reproduced or transmitted in any form or by any means,
electronic or mechanical, including photocopying, recording or by any
information storage and retrieval system, without permission in writing
from the Publisher.
Macmillan Publishing Co., Inc. 866 Third Avenue, New York, N.Y. 10022
Collier-Macmillan Canada Ltd.
Library of Congress catalog card number: 73–19056
Printed in the United States of America

10 9 8 7 6 5 4 3 2 1

The three-color illustrations were prepared as black pencil-and-wash
drawings with overlays for yellow and brown. The typeface is Alphatype
Bookman, with the display set in Melior Semibold.

Library of Congress Cataloging in Publication Data
Prather, Ray.   No trespassing.
I. Title.   PZ7.P887NO   [E]   73–19056   ISBN 0-02-775020-5

To Robert and Laura Russ—
Big Pa and Big Ma

"Look, there it is, Willie Jr. See it?
Under that bush."

"Yes, but be quiet, Jay.

Miss Riley might hear us."

"Hi, what're you guys looking at?"

"Shhh...scram, runt, or you'll get us caught."

"Don't call me runt and don't tell me to scram, or I'll holler."

"Okay, Charlie, but we're busy."

"No, we're not, Willie Jr. Want to do us a favor, Charlie?"

"What kind of favor, Jay?"

"See that ball, Charlie?"

"You think I'm crazy. Miss Riley's a witch."

"Come on, Charlie, you'll be in and out in no time."

"Hurry up, Charlie.
Under that bush.
Come on, hurry it up!"

"You little devil!

   What're you doing in my yard?

   Just wait until I get my hands on you."

"RUN, Charlie. RUN!"

"Quick, head over to Willie Jr.'s house.
  We'll double back later."
"She calls those old weeds flowers."
"Did she spot the ball, Charlie?"
"No, I don't think so.
  But she's got eyes like a hawk."
"She sure looks like one too, huh Jay?"

"Willie Jr., where's your daddy's fishing pole?"

"What's that got to do with your ball?"

"Just get it and I'll show you."

"Get down and stay low."

"Charlie, stay behind Willie Jr.—and no talking."

"Well, look who's brave now."

"I said no talking, Charlie."

"Can you reach it, Jay?"

"No, it's not long enough."

"Well, what're we going to do now?"

"Be quiet. I'm thinking."

"Charlie...."

"Don't look at me, Jay.

 I'm not going back in there no more."

"Willie Jr...."

"Me neither, Jay. Don't look over here. You go."

"Well, find me a long stick, Willie Jr., and give me your handkerchief.

"What do you want with my handkerchief, Jay?"

"Just give it to me, chicken, and be quiet."

"Oops...the stick broke."

"That was my daddy's fishing pole, Jay."

"I know that, Willie Jr."

"We've got to crawl through that old fence."

"What do you mean 'we,' Jay?"

"You hit my ball over there, didn't you?"

"But you dropped my daddy's pole."

"Shhh…

old lady Riley's coming."

"Did she see us?"

"No, but she sure saw that pole."

"HEY MISS RILEY, HEY MISS RILEY.
  SOMEBODY'S IN THE BACKYARD STEALING YOUR PEACHES.
  HEY MISS RILEY, HEY MISS RILEY."

"Quick, through the fence, Willie Jr.

She's in the backyard.

Grab the pole. I'll get the ball."

"That was real neat, Charlie. Right, Willie Jr.?
   How'd you think of it?"

"Oh, I saw it on TV."

"Wow, man."

"Want to play ball with us, Charlie? You can hit
   if you want to. But watch where you hit."